Eye in the Sky

Janice Marriott

illustrated by Donna Cross

Learning Media

Chapter 1

Ali went to the magic store to buy a hairy hand for her big brother's birthday. She wanted to buy him something awful because he was going to a party that night but she wasn't allowed to go.

At the magic store, Ali bought an eyeball instead. Why? Because she liked the way it looked at her. It was a large, round eyeball with tasteful, red veins and clots painted on it and a few yellow lumps on the light brown iris.

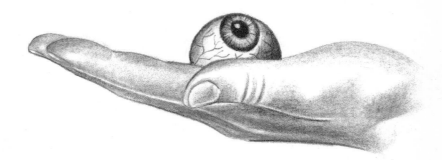

"Don't wrap it, thanks." She liked the way it nestled into her palm.

Ali carried the eyeball back along Lincoln Street to the green apartment building with red grilles where she lived. Her brother was in the kitchen staring into the open fridge.

"Turn around," she said. "I've bought you a hairy hand."

"Ha, ha," Damon said, staring at the eye clenched between Ali's teeth. She saw him jump, just a small shudder of fear. Great!

"That's dumb. I wish you'd gotten me a hairy hand. Anything but that." Then he spun around and began unscrewing the lids off ancient jars in the back of the fridge.

Ali spat the eyeball onto the kitchen counter. "Olives, yum!" she shouted over Damon's shoulder as he squatted to look at the bottom shelf. She tried to grab the olives, but he grabbed the jar away from her.

"No one could like those," he said.

"I love them."

"No way," Damon said. He grabbed the eyeball, dropped it into the olive jar, and screwed the lid back on. The eyeball gazed at Ali from out of the dark liquid.

"Give it to me!"

"No!"

In the middle of the fight, their mother came into the kitchen carrying a pile of flattened cardboard cartons. "Stop that!" she said. "I've got to get ten cartons of food out to a client in the next five minutes. Help me or get out of my way!"

Damon unscrewed the lid and offered an olive to his mom. "Have one," he said. "They're delicious."

She reached for the jar without looking, took one, and raised it to her mouth. She had picked the eyeball. It stared straight at her. She looked at it. She screamed and threw the eyeball out through the open window, sending it arcing across the blue sky above the traffic on Lincoln Street.

Chapter 2

Marco was walking along Lincoln Street to get rid of the bad feeling he got from riding in the back seat on long car trips. His dad had driven him and his big brother Gabe for hours and hours to get to this strange, big city where Gabe lived. Gabe had been home on vacation, and he'd thought it'd be a great idea for Marco to stay with him in the city for a few days. But the idea had been dumb. The trip had been boring. And the worst part of it was that Marco had had to sit in the back seat.

He was still smarting with the injustice of the back-seat car journey – no control, nothing to do, cramped legs, unable to see the road ahead because his father's and brother's heads were in the way, unable to see the scenery because it streaked past the side windows as a blur, having to listen to Gabe's country and western music. The memories were painful. Life was painful. Nothing good ever happened to Marco.

And the worst thing of all had been that his father wouldn't stop for any food. He'd handed out soggy sandwiches and warm orange juice. So, now, on Lincoln Street, Marco was hungry, real hungry. He looked along the road, past a green apartment building with red grilles, to what looked like a donut store. Great! That looked like the right kind of place.

But he never got there. Right at that moment, an eyeball flew out of a window above him.

Eddie Kaslow was walking slowly and carefully along Twelfth Avenue toward Lincoln Street. There seemed to be too many people in the world, and they were all moving too fast. He was walking in a welcome home parade, behind a loud brass band, and his ears hurt from the noise.

The parade was for him – Eddie Kaslow – the spaceman who'd landed back on Earth a few days ago. He'd been in orbit for a year. He wasn't used to the chaos on Earth. He still thought he saw small round objects circling through space whenever he looked up. So Eddie didn't look up. He put one weak leg in front of the other, tried to focus his blurry eyes, and hoped he'd get through the city's welcome to him without doing anything too dumb.

Meanwhile Ali's mom turned on her. "I am tired of your stupid jokes!"

"Me? It was him."

"It's not my eyeball," laughed Damon. He whistled a tune, raised his eyebrows at their mother, and wandered off.

Ali was speechless at the unfairness of it all. She wished she could get back at him.

"Now, Ali, I need your help to get all this food into the elevator and down to the van."

"Nothing good ever happens to me," Ali screamed at her astonished mother as she ran out of the apartment.

Ali had a mission – to get the eyeball back. It was all she could think about. In the few minutes she'd owned the eyeball, she'd become very fond of it. She raced to the elevator and stabbed at the button. The light on the top of the board stared at her, indicating it was on the top floor. Slowly it came down, down, nine, eight, seven … stop. The door opened, and Ali hurled herself in.

In one corner of the elevator was old Mrs. Chan, who liked sailing up and down in the elevator, stopping at each floor and peering out along the corridors, just nosing around. Ali looked at the buttons. All of them had been pressed. That meant that the elevator would stop on every floor. She stamped her feet. She refused to speak to Mrs. Chan. There was nothing she could do to prevent the very slow elevator from stopping at every floor.

By the fifth floor, it was unbearable being in the elevator with Mrs. Chan. The eyeball could have landed anywhere. It might even have been run over by a car.

Ali flung herself out of the elevator and ran down the stairs.

Around down, around down. Around down, around down. Around down, around down. Around down, around down. Around down, around down ....

She got dizzier and dizzier.

Chapter 3

When Marco looked up into the sky, he didn't notice anything unusual, just clouds and buildings that seemed to be leaning in as if they were peering down at him, a little speck way below them. He didn't even notice the people he nearly bumped into. He was too busy concentrating on his new design idea – a plan for the perfect car for kids to ride in. Just an idea, something for a perfect world.

First, the seats in the back would be sleeker and more luxurious than those in the front. Marco's palms and fingertips tingled as he thought about the soft leather covering the seats. There'd be more legroom for the back-seat passengers and room for at least one dog. There'd also be a fridge stocked with food and drink.

On the back of the driver's seat, there'd be a master panel with controls for the air conditioning, the music, and the seats. At the touch of a button, glass screens would slide up between the driver's half of the car and the back seat so that kids could have private conversations and play their own music. There'd be Internet access from a screen folding down from the roof and headsets with virtual reality games.

Bigger, better ideas came to Marco – an ignition lock would operate from the back seats so that the car would only start if you wanted it to and the driver could only take you where you wanted to go.

He imagined the TV commercial: "*The Blissan Dreamer has an ultraresponsive, overhead cam V8 engine, a balanced, rear-wheel-drive chassis, and a double wishbone suspension that guarantees no wobble or drink spillage during a ride that feels as rich and smooth as melted chocolate. Goodbye, car sickness. The all-new, all-aluminum, 3.2-liter, 24-valve engine delivers 225 horsepower, so it can outrun the fastest animal – even a cheetah.*"

Marco was so engrossed in his ideas that he nearly fell into the gutter. This jerked him back into reality. He was able to imagine things so clearly that he often had difficulty adjusting back to the real world. The world in his head was so much better, but he'd never worked out how to make the dream world real. He knew that the dream car would always be just that – a dream.

"I wish," said Marco to some passersby, "I could meet a car designer." The passersby stared at him. To avoid their stare, he looked up.

At that moment, he saw something flying through the sky. What was it? An eyeball? What the …? It seemed as real as the leather seat covers that he'd just imagined. Was that eyeball real? How could it be?

The eyeball whizzed over Marco's head as the brass band came around the corner onto Lincoln Street. Eddie Kaslow was feeling dazed and other-worldly, stumbling along behind the band. Nothing on Earth looked real to him at that moment. The only thing that felt real was that he was hungry, and there'd be a feast when the parade was over. One year of being in space and his craving for steak was way out of control. "I wish, I wish," he kept saying out loud. Inside his head he kept chanting, "One small step for Eddie, one giant step nearer to the food."

The eyeball plummeted down, down. A trumpeter in the first row of the brass band was waving his trumpet around, getting into the swing. He tilted the trumpet up as he went for a difficult note. The eyeball fell straight down the throat of that trumpet. One moment the trumpet was playing the notes of *Polly Wolly Doodle,* and the next there was silence. The purple-faced trumpet player blew and blew for all he was worth, but no sound came out at all.

The band members were well trained. They kept marching forward, tubas doing lots of oompahs, drums pounding, and cymbals clashing. The trumpet player kept blowing, his face getting more and more purple. Then, suddenly, the trumpet made a shriek that lasted four whole bars and got higher and higher in pitch. It brought the whole band to a crashing, clanging halt. The second row of saxophones rammed into the necks of the front row of brass players. The drums shunted into the backs of the horns. Musicians swiveled around and jabbed each other with their instruments. Drum sticks were raised. Tubas swung dangerously.

The spaceman fell into the back of the biggest drummer. He got up, dusted himself down, and tried to look like a hero again.

While this chaos was happening, Marco watched as the thing that looked like an eyeball whooshed out of the trumpet at great speed, straight up into the blue sky, up, up, up, until Marco could hardly see it. It could have been a bumble bee buzzing in the air. He stepped backward, gazing upward, not taking his eyes off the tiny black dot and – crash! He banged straight into …

Chapter 4

... **A**li!

She had stumbled dizzily out of her green apartment building. She'd tottered into the street and looked up to see what everyone was staring at in the blue sky. The clouds were swirling around and around, circling a tiny black dot – a fly perhaps?

She stepped back to stop herself falling over, and – crash! She went smack into the back of some guy.

They both fell to the ground. He got up first. As she lay there, gazing upward, she saw the black dot get bigger and bigger as it fell through the sky toward them. Yes! It was her eyeball! She staggered up, desperate to catch it before it smashed to pieces on the ground.

She tottered, swayed, righted herself, and saw the parade hero pushing band members out of the way. He strode two paces to the left, held out his large hand, and caught the eyeball. Not bad for someone who hadn't been able to practice ball skills in a year. He beamed and, for a second, looked confident and powerful, the way that spacemen are meant to look.

Eddie looked down at his hand. He opened it slowly. An eye glared straight at him from his palm. The spaceman totally freaked out. He gave a very high, feeble yell, dropped the eyeball into the gutter, and fled. He ran across Lincoln Street, down a side street, and disappeared. That was the end of the parade. No hero, no parade.

As the media pack raced after him to find out why the spaceman had suddenly run away, Marco swept the eyeball up into his pocket and ran off, back the way he'd come, forgetting his hunger for a moment.

Ali took off after him.

Marco headed back to his brother's place, an old communal house on Seventh Avenue. He'd had enough of the big city for a while. It was too unpredictable. His brother was out. Great. He needed a bit of time on his own. He put the eyeball on the table beside him, turning it so that the eye was watching him, then lay on the bed he guessed he'd be sleeping in that night. He fed a CD into his Walkman and chilled out.

He didn't know that Ali was watching him through the window. She had crept around the side of the house and peered through the windows until she found Marco's room. When Marco lay down, she thought she'd be in for a boring spy session. But after a bit the door opened, and a guy came into the room. He was older but looked like the dude on the bed.

"Got caught in some parade. Traffic's banked up. Streets closed. Some spaceman in town. Marco, are you listening?"

"Yeah. What, like an alien from space or someone from here who's been there?"

"Dunno."

"Aha."

"You've got to write to Mom."

Marco got up and began writing at Gabe's desk: Dear Mom, We arrived after a safe trip. Nothing much has happened so far. I saw an eyeball fall out of the sky. I nearly met a famous spaceman. Love, Marco.

"Hey, Gabe, any food in this place?" Marco asked when he'd finished the letter.

"Ah, no. I haven't gotten any in yet. The parade really messed things up. I'll go get some."

When the older guy opened the front door, Ali rushed in while pretending to fumble for her key. She stood in the hallway and peered into the room where she'd seen Marco. Ali watched him drawing at a small desk. She could see the eyeball on the table beside him, watching him. He was too engrossed in his work to notice.

Marco started on another drawing. He was thinking detail now. This car would have a premium, six-speaker sound system, power windows, and door locks operated from the back-seat, master control panel. It would have seat belts with so many controls on them that they'd be like wearable computers. You could lie back, press a keypad on your seat belt and go real cool places, like space, jungles, and dinosaur swamps. The driver would be like a chauffeur.

Marco began a third drawing of the car pointing upward into the sky from Lincoln Street. He drew in the band members, who were surrounding the car, all staring upward. "Optional extra," he heard the voice-over of the TV commercial. "Vertical takeoff and landing capability to get you out of uncool situations." Why not? In this city world, anything was possible. After a while, he'd had enough, so he lay down and went to sleep.

Ali crept in to pick up her eyeball. As she reached out for it, she saw the drawings. There was a car – unlike any car she'd ever seen.

It had a small hood, a radiator, and headlights, and the wheel arches at the back were like the back legs of a panther about to spring. The whole car was like a panther. It seemed alive as if it was about to leap up, to spring, to bend. It was an extraordinary drawing. More real than the real thing, because the real thing was impossible.

She picked up the drawings. Marco stirred. Ali ran, the drawings still in her hand.

She had no time to pick up the eyeball. When she fled through the open door, Ali glanced back, and her eyes locked on the eyeball. It watched her leave.

Chapter 5

Marco woke to the eyeball's threatening stare. "Awwk," he said in the empty room and turned it away.

He got up. He searched for the drawings on the desk. They had vanished. Weird. Things that weren't supposed to happen did happen in this strange place.

Marco's brother arrived back with two videos, but no food, and turned on the TV. "Hey, it's that band. Look! After they turned the corner into Lincoln, seems they rioted or something. Who's that guy running away? It looks like the spaceman, Eddie Kaslow. But it can't be. Hey! Look! That's you! The one bending down, over there!"

Marco got up to look, but the item had ended, and a commercial for washing powder came on the screen.

"Man! You were on TV!" shouted his brother, looking at Marco with new respect.

"So?" muttered Marco, slouching back to the desk.

Marco couldn't draw with Gabe around. He added a note to the letter to his mom: P.S. I was on TV. He put the eyeball and the letter in his pocket and went out in search of food. He headed up Lincoln Street toward the donut store.

Eddie Kaslow, the once-famous spaceman, was quietly sipping a drink in a café, trying to be invisible. It was easy for him to go unnoticed because most people only recognized him when he had a spacesuit on and they couldn't see his face. Strange world, he thought. The TV started broadcasting the parade. He watched in horror as the cameras zoomed in on him standing triumphantly with one arm stretched out, fist tightly closed. Then the camera showed him running away. Total humiliation, thought Eddie. No amount of years in space will make up for this.

Then he watched as the footage showed a boy scoop an eyeball out of the gutter and put it in his pocket. And you could see clearly that the thing he scooped up really was an eyeball! Not that anyone else watching had noticed that. Because they weren't expecting to see body parts raining down from the skies. But if we could just freeze-frame that bit, he thought.

See, I told you so, he wanted to yell to everyone in the café. He had proof now that there really was an eyeball out there, haunting him. He gulped down the rest of his drink and left. He walked back to Lincoln Street, in search of the boy so that he could make him tell the nation how an eyeball had come to fall from the sky into the spaceman's hand.

"That boy," Eddie muttered, "holds the key to my sanity and my reputation."

Ali arrived home, and as she walked through the living room, she turned on the TV. She saw the footage of the parade chaos. The band members were standing around accusing each other of having stopped playing. The hero was declared by in-studio experts to have an antiparade problem due to being in space too long. There were shots of a huge and very empty marquee with tables lined with food. Her mom was standing grimly by a large ice sculpture shaped like a panther.

"So that was the function Mom was catering for."

Ali sat down and took out the car drawings. She stared at them for a long time. She noticed that the boy had drawn, on the dashboard inside the car, her eyeball. It was staring out at the road ahead, as though it were doing the driving.

Her mother burst into the apartment, and Ali jumped.

"My function's ruined!" yelled her mom. "That space hero ran out."

"I know. I saw it on TV." Then she realized that she knew, not because she'd seen it on TV but because she'd actually been there when the band had stopped playing and had seen the spaceman catch the eyeball and run away.

"He was freaked out by my eyeball," she said.

Her mom ignored the remark because it didn't make sense. "You talk such nonsense. All I know is that all that food is going to waste." She switched the TV off just as a psychologist was creating a personality profile of the hero. The hero disappeared from their room, like a genie vanishing back into a bottle.

The phone rang. Ali's mom picked it up, muttered "Aha. Aha." a few times, and then slammed it down. "I have to save that food," she said. "Come on!"

"No, I can't. I've got to get my eyeball."

"Don't be ridiculous!" shouted her stressed-out mother. "You're coming with me."

Ali had no choice. She was dragged out to help pack up the food. She just had time to stuff the panther-like car drawings back in her pocket.

"Hi, Mrs. Chan. Fancy seeing you here," said Ali as she got in the elevator.

She felt strangely incomplete. She wished she hadn't left the eyeball behind in that boy's room. She wanted to be with it. It felt like it was part of her.

The elevator bumped to a halt. Ali and her mom stepped out onto Lincoln Street's busy sidewalk.

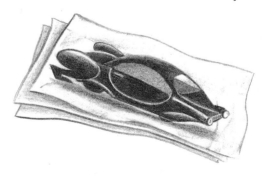

Chapter 6

As Marco walked past the big glass doors of the green apartment building, he groped in his pocket for the eyeball. He found it and a ball of string and started juggling them to help his car ideas flow. Although he was a good juggler, the eyeball kept slipping through his fingers and rolling onto the sidewalk. It rolled further than he expected it to. He had to run after it.

He was reaching for it when a girl came at him out of nowhere.

"That's mine!"

"Mine!"

Ali and Marco stared hard into each other's eyes. They both stepped back one pace.

"Aren't you the girl ...?"

"Aren't you the guy ...?" They both spoke at exactly the same time.

"Do you always crash into people as a way of saying 'Hi'?"

"Do you always collide with people?"

Then, they both lunged for the eyeball. Ali grabbed for it just as it rolled toward her. It slipped past her fingertips, and Marco swooped on it. He'd got it!

"Give it back."

"No way."

"Quit fighting, you two," said Ali's mother, striding out of the apartment building.

Marco started walking. Ali and her mom walked with him. Ali shouted, "It is so my eyeball. My mom flung it out the window into the brass band. I saw you pick it up. Give it back!"

Marco's head was reeling. This city was just too weird. "What'll you give me for it?" Marco asked.

Ali thought about it. She couldn't offer the drawings because she'd have to explain how she came to have them. While she wondered what this strange boy would like, her mother said, "What about all the food you can eat – for free?"

Marco stared at Ali. Could these people read his mind? Was this a real city he'd fetched up in, or was he in a virtual city, like in a computer game? "One eyeball in exchange for lots of food," he said.

"A deal."

They both laughed.

Marco handed the eyeball over. Ali took off after her mom, who was disappearing between the huge buildings.

"Hey, wait up," yelled Marco.

Just then, Eddie Kaslow was puffing up Lincoln Street. He looked worried. Could he really be going mad? He'd been warned in training sessions that sometimes it's hard to adjust to being back on Earth. But no one had told him that he'd catch an eyeball. How would he know what was real if some of the things he saw were just too weird?

He ran as fast as he could, but his muscles weren't coping with Earth's gravity. Puff. Puff. He was getting slower and slower. His eyes were swinging left and right. Behind him was a pack of media hounds, throwing questions at him as they came. "Why did you run away?" "Was a year in space too much for you?" "Have you accepted any film offers?"

Then Eddie saw Marco. "That's the kid!" he roared, or tried to roar. A tiny squeak came out. "That's ... the kid ...," he gasped, "who took the eyeball .... He'll show you it's real," he spluttered. "Ask him."

The media pack surrounded Marco. He couldn't move. His chance of catching up with the mother and daughter free-food dispensers was blown.

Just my luck, thought Marco.

Chapter 7

"You! I need you!" shouted Eddie.

"Aren't you the famous spaceman, sir?"

"That's me. Eddie K, the spaceman."

Right, thought Marco. You're like, real famous. You want me? I'm obviously in a dream. Now I think of it, everything today's been like a dream. Maybe I'm still in Dad's car. When I wake up ….

"So what task do you want me to undertake?" he asked the spaceman, as grandly as he could.

"I want that eyeball!" shouted Eddie.

"I haven't got it."

Eddie Kaslow groaned. The media hooted and clapped and laughed.

"He's got space madness. Worst case I've seen," said the space correspondent from the *New York Times* into his cell phone. Eddie Kaslow seemed to shrivel up in front of Marco. Marco felt sorry for him.

"Look, mister, I think I'm in a virtual reality computer game or a dream or something. This place is too weird. But I'll give you the facts as I know them. One: I can't get you your eyeball because I gave it to a girl in exchange for food. Two: The girl's gone after her mother who was making food for you at the city welcome."

"Let's go then!" spluttered Eddie.

"I don't know where that is."

"The welcome's in the park. Follow me," said Eddie.

"Sure thing," Marco said, and they both took off down alleys and across roads, followed by a bunch of journalists babbling into their cell phones.

Around the next corner was a large park. In the park was a huge marquee, and in the marquee was a vast amount of food. Definitely a computer game, thought Marco, and I must be winning.

The table in front of them was piled with little pies, sausage kebabs, sushi, and a huge platter of glittering black stuff on crackers.

"Chocolate!" shouted Marco. They both reached for a cracker. Marco put a whole one in his mouth. "Yuck!" He spat it out.

"Caviar," explained the spaceman. "Nah! What we want is steak and fries!"

"There!" shouted Marco, and they both ran to the middle of the marquee where a barbecue was glowing.

As they ate steak with onions and bacon, and a small mountain of fries, the spaceman grew in confidence.

"Now, show me the girl with the eyeball," he roared.

Marco looked up at the rapidly filling marquee. Where was the girl? How would he find her? People were jostling each other, keen to get close to the famous spaceman who had magically reappeared. This unplanned way of getting to the welcome made him more interesting rather than less. There was lots of pushing and shoving. "I don't know," shouted Marco. "I can't see."

The spaceman hoisted him up onto his shoulders. "Look, boy, look!"

Then Marco saw her. She was staring straight at him but talking to an old dude with white hair. "There!" shouted Marco. "At two o'clock or north-northeast, at a guess."

"Your quest is to reach her," yelled the spaceman.

They plowed through the crowd, with a comet tail of journalists frantic to get the photo opportunity they'd always dreamed of. They got closer and closer. Ali saw Marco. Marco saw Ali. He climbed down from the spaceman's shoulders.

"Sorry to trouble you," Marco started, suddenly feeling shy talking to this cool city girl. "I wondered if you could show the spaceman the eyeball so he can show it to the photographers so they'll believe him when he explains why he ran away from the parade."

She smiled. She took the eyeball out of her pocket, and a million flashbulbs lit up around them. Everyone cheered. A thousand microphones, like fossilized ice-cream cones, were suspended in front of the trio.

The spaceman was interviewed: "I couldn't have done it without this boy."

Marco was interviewed: "The spaceman is the best catcher I've seen."

Ali was interviewed: "My mom did the catering."

After the photos had been taken, the interviews had been recorded, and the journalists had left, the man who Ali had been talking to bent down and picked up the pieces of paper that had fluttered out of Ali's pocket when she'd taken out the eyeball. He smoothed them out and looked at them. He asked Ali where she'd got the drawings from.

"Never seen them before, Dad," she snapped quickly.

"They're mine!" Marco said. "Where did you get them?"

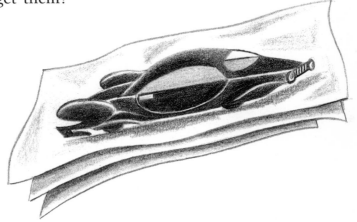

Chapter 8

Marco looked up into five, light brown eyes. Ali's, her father's, and the eyeball.

"This is remarkable," Ali's father said. "The best car sketches I've seen in years. They have power. They're unforgettable. And that's what we're always looking for."

"Shut up, Dad," Ali said, looking embarrassed.

"You … er … want them?" stammered Marco.

"Here's my card," said her father. "I'm in advertising. Car commercials are my speciality. I'd like to see more like this. So refreshingly different and … er …."

"Unforgettable?" asked Marco.

"Absolutely."

They stared at each other. Then Marco asked the question he just had to ask: "Are you a car designer, sir?"

Ali's father laughed. "No. But I deal with them, of course. Big time. Call me tomorrow. We mustn't let that talent go to waste, huh?"

"My teacher says it's doodling."

"Garbage! You keep that card safe. Call me tomorrow!"

"I will, sir."

The spaceman wandered up with a tray of prawns and a chili dipping sauce. "Hey, kid, you wanna come out west sometime and check out our base. Maybe watch a rocket launch? I owe you one. Here's my number. Call me. You're a hero." He lurched forward to give Marco a hug. Marco didn't want to end up stuck to a thousand prawns, so he neatly side-stepped him.

Marco's dreams were coming true. He could call a famous spaceman anytime, and tomorrow he was going to meet someone who was interested in his car ideas. What an unreal day.

"Hey, boy, wrap your face around this prawn!" The spaceman waved the plate in front of him again. "Haven't had decent seafood for so long," he moaned.

"I guess not," said Marco. Suddenly he felt sick. It was all becoming too much. He ran out of the marquee, through the alleys, across the road, to the now-familiar Lincoln Street, where the skies are blue and eyeballs fly through them and dreams seem to come true. He went into the donut store.

"I started the day wanting to get to this donut store, and now my wish has come true," he said to the old man behind the counter. He ordered a cup of hot chocolate. It came in a mug with a handle shaped like an ear. The ear was hot to touch.

He added another note to his letter at the table by the window.

Mom, the spaceman's invited me to check out a rocket launcher. I think I have a job in an advertising agency drawing cars. I ate steak and prawns for dinner, and caviar, but I didn't like that. That's all for now. Will write again if I have any news. Love, Marco.

He went outside to post the letter and discovered a magic store next door. He went inside.

Ali returned home to find her brother getting ready for his big night out.

"Ali! Check my tie. Is it all right?"

She looked at the knot of his tie and then at his hands resting loosely on his shirt front. She stared. She stared again. Between his fingers, hairs had started to sprout.

Ali felt for the eyeball in her pocket. It was warm to her touch. She was beginning to realize something impossible but real and totally wonderful. She didn't plan to tell anyone because no one would believe her. But she thought she'd just go somewhere quiet and draw up a list of things she'd like to make happen.

Hmmm, I'll do that at the donut store, she thought, and then I'll go into the magic store and see what else they have for sale.